THE REVEREND THOMAS'S FALSE TEETH

RETOLD BY GAYLE GILLERLAIN
PICTURES BY DENA SCHUTZER

BridgeWater Paperback

Text copyright © 1995 by Gayle Gillerlain.
Illustrations copyright © 1995 by Dena Schutzer.

Published by BridgeWater Paperback, an imprint and trademark
of Troll Communications L.L.C.

First published in hardcover by BridgeWater Books.

First paperback edition published 1997.

Printed in the United States of America.

10 9 8 7 6 5 4 3 2 1

Library of Congress Cataloging-in-Publication Data
Gillerlain, Gayle.
The Reverend Thomas's false teeth / Gayle Gillerlain;
illustrated by Dena Schutzer.
p.   cm.
Summary: On his way to have dinner with Gracie and her family, the preacher
loses his teeth in the Chesapeake Bay.
ISBN 0-8167-3303-1 (lib. bdg.) ISBN 0-8167-3304-X (pbk.)
[1. Teeth--Fiction 2. Chesapeake Bay (Md. and Va.)—Fiction.]
I. Schutzer, Dena, ill.   II. Title.
PZ7.G402Re   1995   [E]—dc20   93-39980

To Rick and John,
with thanks for your support and encouragement.
G.G.

For my first art teacher,
Joseph Presser.
D.S.

A long time ago, on the Eastern Shore of the Chesapeake Bay, there lived a girl named Gracie. On this particular afternoon Gracie was setting the table. She was trying to do a 'specially good job because the Reverend Thomas was coming to dinner.

Mama had cooked his favorite fried chicken and was just taking a pie out of the oven. The aromas that floated in from the kitchen made Gracie's stomach growl with hunger. As she placed the last fork on the table, Gracie declared that Preacher Thomas could not walk through the door soon enough to suit her.

Suddenly the door flew open.
Gracie's brother Will burst in.
"Daddy, come quick," he called.
"The Reverend Thomas has lost
his false teeth overboard."

Daddy rushed off with Will. Mama and Gracie followed. The family hurried down to the pier with a dozen curious neighbors trailing behind. There stood the Reverend Thomas, praying for the safe return of his lost teeth.

As soon as he said "Amen," the people all started talking at once. "How did it happen?" they asked. "What can we do? We have to get Preacher Thomas's teeth back before some mean ol' jimmy-crab makes off with them."

"I know how to get his teeth," announced Gracie.

"Be quiet, Gracie," said Will. "I'll get them." He took a deep breath and jumped into the water. Twice he came up for air and swam back down to look for the teeth. He looked until his eyes stung from the salt water, but he could not find them. Finally Will gave up.

"That was a brave try, Will," the Reverend Thomas said.

Gracie pulled on her mother's sleeve. "Mama, I know how to get his teeth," she said.

"Hush now, honey. Let us think," Mama said softly.

A man spoke up, "I'll bet we could scoop them up with a crab net."

Several boys raced off. Soon they returned carrying crab nets. The Reverend Thomas and the others gathered around.

The boys pulled the nets through the water and dragged them along the bottom. Time after time they raised the nets only to find them empty or holding the wrong catch.

"Thank you, boys," said the Reverend Thomas.
"I know you did your best." He tried to look calm,
but his forehead began to wrinkle with worry.

"I know how to get his teeth," Gracie said again, hoping someone would listen to her. No one paid her any mind, so off she ran toward her house. "I'll show them," she declared.

"We'll have to try tonging up those teeth," said Gracie's dad. He and some other men fetched their oyster tongs. They worked the heavy tongs over and over— lower, open, close, lift.

They brought up five bottles, an old shoe, and a mess of oyster shells, but no teeth.

"Thank you, brothers," said the Reverend Thomas.

"I don't know what else we can do," said Gracie's dad. No one else did either.

Just then Gracie walked up holding one end of a length of string. The other end was hidden in her apron pocket. She took something from the pocket and threw it out over the water.

The string unfurled, and *plop,* the thing it was tied to dropped into the water. After only a few minutes she pulled in the string.

There, clamped firmly onto the mysterious object, were the Reverend Thomas's false teeth. "How did you do that?" the people wanted to know. "What's on that string?"

"At the big picnic Preacher Thomas said he could not keep his teeth out of good fried chicken, so I used Mama's chicken for bait," Gracie explained.

Everyone got a good laugh from that.

Preacher Thomas popped his store-bought teeth back into his mouth.

"Thank you all for your help," the Reverend Thomas said, "especially you, Gracie. You out-thought us all. Shall we go have dinner now? The rest of my mouth wants to taste that chicken."

Gracie and her family walked
the Reverend Thomas to the house.
There they all gave thanks…

and sank their teeth into a delicious fried chicken
dinner at a 'specially well-set table.